Also by Geraldine McCaughrean

Doctor Quack

Six Storey House

Dog Days

For older readers, Geraldine
McCaughrean's prize-winning retelling
of the classic tale by John Bunyan:

Pilgrim's Progress

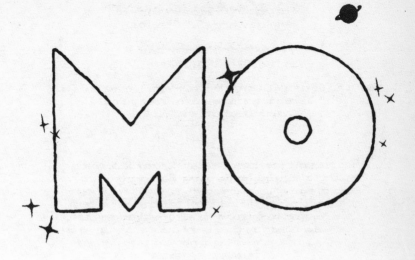

Geraldine McCaughrean

ILLUSTRATED BY ROSS COLLINS

Hodder
Children's
Books

a division of Hodder Headline Limited

Printed and bound in Great Britain
by Clays Ltd, St Ives plc

The paper and board used in this paperback by Hodder Children's Books
are natural recyclable products made from wood grown in
sustainable forests. The manufacturing processes conform to the
environmental regulations of the country of origin.

Hodder Children's Books
A division of Hodder Headline Limited
338 Euston Road, London NW1 3BH

For more information about the author please visit:
www.geraldinemccaughrean.co.uk

For KRISTINA and KELI SULAJ
with love

Contents

Chapter One
No Phones

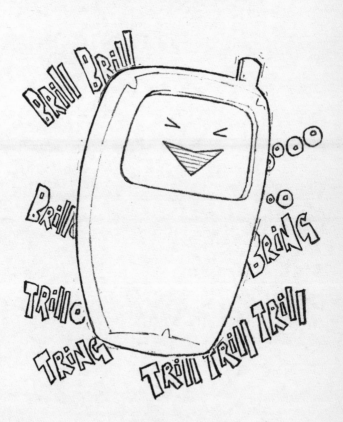

Somewhere a phone was ringing. It started softly – a tootling, footling tune – but it got louder. Soon the whole corridor was full of chirpy chirruping. Even in the hall, where everyone was at assembly, the ringing could be heard loud and clear:

Brill! Brill!

"I do hope nobody has brought their mobile phone into school," said the Head Teacher in shocked tones. "You all know what I have said: mobile phones must be left at home."

Trill! Trill! Trill!

"Shane: please go and find that telephone – wherever it is – and bring it to me," said the Head.

Why did she choose Shane? Who knows? Perhaps she knew him

to be an intrepid explorer and a fearless sleuth. Perhaps she saw that he had exceptional earsight. Perhaps she (secretly) thought of Shane as her trusty sidekick.

Or perhaps she chose him because he was sitting next to the door.

Shane was startled. He had been far away – imagining – being an explorer or a sleuth or a deputy. But now even he could hear the phone ringing in the corridor:

Trillo! Trillo! Trillo!

Outside the hall, the corridor stretched away into the distance. Along each wall hung coats and macks. The whole passageway was quilted with coats, but even they did not soak up the sound.

Thrill! Thrill! Thrill!

Under some of the coats stood wellington boots. It was as if Shane was walking between a guard-of-honour – or running the last leg of a big race with cheering spectators on either side. He jogged down the corridor, giving a cheery wave to the cheering crowds.

Thrillo! Thrillo! Thrillo!

The noise was so loud now that it hurt his ears. He must be getting close. Here were the coats of Class Two. Here was where Class Three threw their outdoor clothing at the hooks and let most of it fall on the floor.

Shane hoped the phone did not belong to anyone he knew: they would be in big trouble with the Head. He hoped the phone did not belong to Bagless Dyson or Knees Nelson or Wapper Harris. It was not Shane's fault he had been sent to find the phone, but Bagless and Knees and Wapper could be very unreasonable.

Gorillo! Gorillo! Gorillo!

Oddly, the phone seemed to be tootling a different tune now . . .

Here were the Class Four coats. Here were the gloves his friend Chiller hated so much because they were attached to his sleeves by tapes. Here was Maggie's pink bomber jacket and Millie's anorak and Smiler's mack. So it must be someone in his own class who . . .

Brilliant! Brilliant! Brilliant!

Shane wondered why people were not designed with zips on their ears. If ears had zips, they could be shut when phones rang too loudly for comfort.

Here was Shane's own anorak, facing the wall, as if it was playing hide-and-seek, counting to twenty. The fur trim on the hood was trembling.

Brylcreem! Brylcreem! Brylcreem!

15

Shane tried the coat's pockets first, then he slid his hand into the hood, but he already knew what he would find.

"Quiet!" he said aloud. "Shut up, will you?"

"*Hello! Hello! Hello!*" chirped the mobile phone.

"Shshsh! Or I'll be in trouble!"

In fact something told Shane that he was already in trouble, up to his neck – which was very unfair, given that he did not even own a phone.

Chapter Two
Freephone

The quickest way to silence the phone was to answer it. "Hello?"

"What kept you? I'm hoarse from calling," said the voice, hoarsely.

"You've got the wrong number."

"Don't be personal . . . Why? What number should I have?"

"I mean it's not me you want. This isn't my phone. I mean I just found it. It was ringing. I was passing. Who did you want to talk to? Who did you expect?"

"I expected someone to answer the phone, that's who," said the voice sharply. "I need a lift."

"Well, I'm not the—"

"You're here, now. We won't say any more about it. Why do you have a pouch on the back of your coat? Is

21

it for carrying your young about?"

Shane glanced quickly round. The caller could obviously see him and his coat – or knew where the phone had been hidden. Was this some elaborate practical joke by Wapper or Knees. Would Bagless poke out his head any moment now, wearing a silly, taunting grin? It must be some kind of mean practical joke.

But the voice on the phone was imperious and teacherly. "Tell me about the pouch."

"It's not a pouch. It's a hood, of course. For my head. When it rains."

"You take your head off when it rains!?" The caller sounded very impressed. "Why doesn't your neck let the rain in?"

Shane scowled at the telephone. That was when he noticed for the first time that it did not have an on/off switch. It must be one of those phones that snaps open to show the keys inside. Shane gave it a sharp flick.

"Don't do that! Physical violence is not clever, you know? How would you like it if somebody did that to you? You ought to be more considerate!" It was definitely not Wapper's voice. In fact it sounded more like a girl.

"Who am I talking to?" said Shane, trying to sound bored with the joke.

"Me. Mo."

"Meemo?"

"No, that's my brother. I'm Mo.

23

Just Mo."

"It can't be me you want: I don't own a phone."

"You do now."

If only Temptation was not so tempting!

For as long as Shane could remember – at least six weeks – he had wanted a mobile phone. Everybody in the world seemed to own one, except him. His mother said, *'You don't need a phone. I didn't have a phone when I was your age.'* But what did that have to do with anything? In her days, nobody had mobile phones; mobile phones had not been invented.

Nobody minds not having something that nobody else has.

Nobody minds not having something because it hasn't been invented yet.

Shane did not mind one bit about his mother having no phone. He minded very much about not having one himself.

If Shane had a mobile then he would be like Wapper and Maggie. He too could whip it out – like a cowboy quick on the draw – like a policeman radioing for back-up – like a millionaire reaching for his wallet.

He had tried many times to talk his mother round, but always, in the end, she just said, *'Too expensive'*. (And when his mother used two-word sentences, it was time to stop arguing.)

"Do you mean it? I can keep this phone? Honest?" said Shane to the voice on the mobile.

"Yep."

"Free?" said Shane, thinking of phone cards, rental, a price.

"AS A BIRD!" said the phone. "They'll never catch me now! . . . So put me back inside your pouch and let's get out of here!"

I'm talking to a telephone, thought

Shane. *Not ON a telephone or OVER a telephone or INTO a telephone. No, I'm talking TO a telephone: a phone with no keys and no off-switch.*

"Mo, you said," said Shane. "Mo the Mobile?"

"From Experimental Planet-Planet."

"Planet-Planet?"

"So good they named it twice."

It was a while before Shane was able to control his fit of coughing and see out of his eyes again. "So you don't . . . actually . . . *belong* to . . . anyone."

"Certainly not. My own phone, me! . . . But if you behave yourself, I'll let you mind me for the time being."

Suddenly Shane's guilty conscience banged like a door in the wind. The Head had sent him on a mission to find the ringing phone. He had to report back to her. Of course he need not tell her where he had found Mo. He need not tell her that Mo was alive and on the run from Planet-Planet. In fact he need not tell her . . .

"It stopped ringing, Miss," said Shane, trying to stick to the truth. "I did look for it. But it stopped ringing." Inside his pocket he could feel the telephone gently vibrating, like a bride on her wedding day.

The Head looked at him, her head on one side. He wondered if she had x-ray vision and could see

the mobile hidden in his pocket.

But Shane told himself he was not *seriously* wicked. He would not use the phone in school. Honest. He wouldn't text during lessons. Honest. He wouldn't use his mobile to make the little kids jealous. No. He would just . . . *mind* Mo.

"*Brylcreem!*" said a little voice nearby, just as if Mo knew what he was thinking.

Chapter Three
Mo Tones

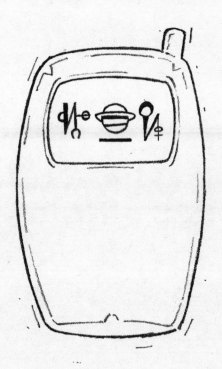

"**So I can't** actually *make a phone call?*" said Shane. It came as a bit of a blow.

"We would be traced," said Mo darkly.

They were in the blanket cupboard outside Shane's bedroom. (Mo worried about radio waves from Shane's computer.) "Anyway, who do you know on Planet-Planet?"

"Do you text, at least?"

"Well of *course* I text," said the mobile with a snort. "You want a text message?" And there it was, instantly, on the little green screen:

ৡ⚲▣⟨⚲⚲Ⳬ⚲⚲⚲⚲⚲⚲⚓

What did it mean? What did it say? Water gurgling out of the bath made as much sense to Shane as this string of signs and symbols.

"I don't understand. Who is it from?"

"From me, of course," said Mo. "Can't you read?"

"Can't you spell?" retorted Shane.

"My spelling is perfect, I'll have you know," said Mo stiffly. "It has often been remarked upon that I have perfect spelling."

"But I . . ."

"Just because you do not speak Lingua Planet-Planet, is it my fault? Do you expect me to use an ALIEN alphabet? In any case, I dare not transmit. Even a text message. They would trace the call. They'd find me."

"They?"

"Them. They're after me."

"*Why?*" said Shane, awash with disappointment. "Why would *anyone* be after you? You're useless, you. You can't take photographs or surf the internet or anything, can you? Admit it! Can you?"

"Surf?" Mo made a gurgling, bubbling, underwater sort of a noise with, here and there, a crackle and a fizz. The whole plastic case trembled, raising Shane's hopes that Mo could vibrate instead of ringing. But Mo was just shuddering at the thought of water.

"What about games?"

"Games?"

"Games."

"I am partial to snooker and football. Not rugby. People bandage over their ears when they play

35

rugby, and I like ears. Telephones like ears. Athletics is amusing. Also intergalactic rowing."

"But *you*, Mo. Don't *you* play any games?"

"Oh *meee*. Well, no. I don't do athletics. I don't have the legs for it. But Chess is stimulating. Bridge. Whist. Mahjong . . ."

Outside on the telegraph wires a blackbird was starting to sing in the evening gloom. Mo warbled gently to herself, trying to find the same key.

"Ring tones!" said Shane, reminded. "Can I set your ring tones, at least."

A mouth appeared on the green screen – a pair of lips curving smugly into more and more of a grin. "My best feature," said the lips. "Mo show."

Mo was justifiably proud of her animal impressions. Not all the animal noises came from Planet-Planet, either. Between the zergong and the hoolybird came a sheep, a cow, a Doberman guard dog and a rhinoceros scratching itself against a tree. Mo had no patience with earthly rock music, but liked opera, especially Bizet. Thanks to her travels, she could also do the noise of bus doors opening and the bleep of a pelican crossing.

"That would be best, I think," said Shane quickly.

Best of all would have been silence. But try as he might, Shane could not make Mo understand: she must keep quiet. He no sooner left Mo in her hiding place and went downstairs than she began to call him back. If he ignored the sheep-bleat or the *March of the Toreadors*, or the hiss of pneumatic brakes, it just got louder and louder. It scared the moths out of the blankets and the starch out of the pillowcases.

"Has someone left the TV on upstairs?" said Shane's dad as family chewing came to a mystified stop around the dinner table.

"I might have," said Shane blushing, and fled upstairs.

When this happened for the third time, Shane's older sister Cora got curious. She followed him up the stairs and found Shane kneeling on the landing, his head deep inside the airing cupboard: *"I keep telling you, Mo! Stop calling me!"*

Cora rested her sharp elbows on his back. "Who are you talking to?" When she saw the mobile phone she

gave a long, low whistle. "Did you steal it?" she said.

"Of course I didn't steal it! I found it. It found me." (It was almost a relief to be found out.) "Look! It's not a proper phone. It comes from Outer Space and it doesn't have an off-switch and you can't make a phone call on it – not even to the Speaking Clock – so it's not so great really. But it talks, you see. It's called Mo and it likes talking. And opera. But not rugby."

It was reckless and foolhardy: to tell the truth, to throw himself on Cora's mercy, to trust her with his secret. But it was a relief. Now someone else would know. Now someone else could take a turn at answering Mo.

Cradled in Shane's hand, Mo glinted in the landing lamplight. A red light pulsed alongside the green screen. For a long time they both sat looking at it.

Meanwhile, Mo the mobile said nothing.

Cora took it and tried to flick it open.

"She doesn't like that!" said Shane hastily. "And she doesn't flick."

But if Mo objected to being flicked, she said nothing. Silence.

"Yep, you stole it," said Cora, nodding her head, agreeing with herself. "That was your accomplice you were talking to before. Now the guilt's driven you mad. Raving mad. Serves you right. Give it back or I'll tell Dad." And Cora banged away downstairs, wearing her most disgusted feet.

"Well?" said Shane, staring at the silent Mo.

"Why does she keep her teeth in a cage?" said Mo trembling ever so slightly.

"It's a brace."

"They must be really fierce teeth, if she has to keep them in a cage!" said Mo.

"I told you . . ."

"Imagine, if they got loose! I wouldn't stand a chance. Not against teeth on the rampage. Horrible. How did she find out they were dangerous? Did they bite a telephone?"

Shane's fingers tightened

around the small alien. If he opened the landing window, he might be able to throw Mo right into next-door's ornamental pond. "You're totally useless, you," he said. "What good are you? No games! No ring-tones! No camera! No phone calls! No texting! Useless!"

It was like being given a toy on Christmas Day without any batteries. It was like being given a pet you are allergic to. It was worse than not having a mobile phone at all.

The small, coffin-shaped moulding of soft warm metal throbbed in his hand and hummed a snatch of ice-cream-van music. Shane thrust Mo between the folds of a big patchwork quilt and slammed shut the airing cupboard door.

"I read the future," said a small, muffled voice through the keyhole. "Does that count?"

Chapter Four
Mo Knows

"There's danger ahead," said Mo.

"Well, of course there is," hissed Shane. "If I get caught with a mobile on me, I'll be toast. So keep your voice down." He hated bringing Mo into school, but he dared not leave her in the airing cupboard, mooing and hissing and singing *Carmen*.

"Danger," said Mo. But then Mo saw danger everywhere. According to Mo, post boxes had their eyes too close together. They were not to be trusted.

"They don't have eyes, Mo."

"So how do they know what to eat and what not to eat?"

"They don't eat, Mo. Post boxes don't eat."

"Don't lie to me! I've seen

47

people feeding them!"

Then there were the supermarket trolleys, huddling together, all in one parking bay in the car park. "They *know*, you see," said Mo darkly. "They know danger is coming."

"I don't believe you can see the future," said Shane flatly. "You get everything else wrong."

So Mo told him which dog would win Crufts World Championship Dog Show the following Saturday.

And it did.

Peerless Brighton III, an English sheepdog, became Champion of Champions (though Mo said that, under all that hair, its eyes were much too close together).

"Pity people can't bet on Crufts," said Shane. "Now if you knew who was going to win the *Derby*, I could have got rich."

And that is how Shane came to know the winner of the Derby even though the Derby was still a week away. Mo told him.

And Shane told Class Four.

He could not help himself.

He could have told his sister Cora, but she would only have said, "So what? *You* can't place a bet at *your* age" – and then gone out and got rich herself. He could always have kept the secret to himself.

But no, Shane blurted it out to Class Four.

He did not say how he knew. He did not say that Mo had told

him. In fact, he did not mention Mo, snuggled up in the hood of his anorak, hidden. "Trust me. I know," was all he said.

Gigi's dad had a betting shop, so Gigi knew very well how to fill in a betting slip. She had been doing it for years. (It was odd that Gigi came bottom in sums, because she was wonderful with numbers.) "If the odds on a horse are 100-to-1 and you bet a pound on it and it wins, you get £100," said Gigi. Class Four gasped.

Some reached for their money at once. Others – like Knees and Bagless – were more careful. They wanted to know how Shane knew who would win the Derby.

"Science," said Shane, tapping

his nose. "I have a system. For reading the Future."

It was playtime and they were all huddled together in Pet Corner where the school rabbits had their hutch. Today there was not much room left for the rabbits.

"Hark at him," sneered Bagless. "Go on then, Shaney. Tell us something that's gonna happen. Tell us a bit of Future!"

So Shane stepped over the low fence and paced about in the playground. He was wearing his anorak back-to-front. Now he began muttering into the hood.

When he came back he said, "Mrs McKeckney will drop her tea mug."

Almost at once there was a

tinkling sound of broken china and a splash. Class Four gaped at Shane, wide-eyed. (He had never shown any sign of doing magic before.)

"Luck," said Bagless sourly. "The next six cars that go by: what colour will they be?" Shane returned to mooching about the playground, mumbling into his hood.

"Boring, boring," said Mo. "Can't you think of something more interesting to ask me? That's just the sort of thing they used to ask me, back on Planet-Planet."

"Red, white, black, silver, silver, black," Shane said when he came back. Twenty-four heads flicked to and fro as the traffic passed by. Even the rabbits seemed to be checking, and rabbits are colour-blind.

"Say where we's going on holiday," said Bagless ferociously.

Shane went back out into the yard. But the answer that Mo whispered, out of the depths of the hood, startled and worried him. "That's wrong, Mo! I know for a fact Bagless is going to Fuengirola. He's been going on about Fuengirola for weeks."

"But he doesn't know his dad will lose his job so they'll have to go to Skegness instead," said Mo impatiently.

Bagless did not like the news about Skegness or his Dad. He chose not to believe it. But everybody else did. It had the ring-tone of truth about it.

By this time, some of Class Four

were experimenting – putting on
their jackets and blazers the wrong
way round, to see if they, too, could
read the Future.

"Who will get told off next,
Shaney?" asked Smiler. "Tell us!"
Off went Shane again, talking to
himself, seeking out the Future like
a water-diviner seeking out water.
"Looks half-witted," said

Chiller, "talking to himself like that."

A moment later, Shane jumped smartly over the fence, scaring the rabbits. "It's me. It's me. It's me!" he

said. His cheeks were red and he was struggling to get his arms out of his sleeves. Mrs McKeckney's voice came drifting after him: ". . . *trouble if I see you wearing your coat the wrong way round again, Shane*

Curry! Stupid boy!"

As Shane hurried to wriggle out of his coat, the little alien phone slid out of the hood and skidded across the ground. The rabbits jumped out of its way. Wapper stopped it with one foot.

"Shaney's got a *mobile."*

It was a jeer, a taunt, a threat-to-tell and a cry of surprise all rolled into one.

"It's not a mobile *actually,"* said Shane, with a casual shrug. (At least it was supposed to look casual. He looked more like a camel with hiccups.) "It's a Futurescope, *actually."* Class Four gave another gasp. "I got it out of the *Innovations* catalogue . . . And the winner of the Derby will be Number Five.

Guaranteed!"

"Don't believe him!"

The voice cut through their chatter, like a fish-slice. A dozen hearts gave a guilty thud of fear. Class Four looked around to see who had spoken.

"Shshsh, Mo!" hissed Shane. Twenty-four pairs of eyes turned on the little alien.

"*Innovations*, indeed!" said Mo indignantly. "I am from Planet-Planet: Experimental model NK/11⊠☐〰 with full Foresee-the-Future facility and a large array of other useful features!" She finished off with the noise of tube-train doors closing and "Mind the Gap!"

*

Everyone brought in one pound, and

Gigi collected the money in a tobacco tin. Thanks to Mo the Clairvoyant Futurescope, they planned to bet it all on Number Five in the Derby and win their fortunes! Even Wapper was convinced.

"You realise this is illegal?" said Smiler. "Betting? At our age?"

Gigi gave a scornful snigger and wrote on the lid of the tin:

"No. 5: TO WIN." She did a few impossible sums in her head and told them they could each expect to win £70.

*

"*Danger!*" said Mo, not for the first time. Mo managed to see more dangers coming than a hedgehog on a motorway.

"I told you, Mo. Stop *worrying*

all the time, will you?"

First it had been the Kit-Kats. Mo had seen Cora eating a Kit-Kat and mistook it for a mobile phone. Shane had to explain: "I told you: you strip off the foil then you eat them. The Kit-Kats don't suffer."

But Mo had moved on from Cora's Kit-Kats.

"Danger! He's going to get me!" said Mo.

"How many times do I have to say, Mo? Nobody's after you! They wouldn't come all the way here from Planet-Planet just to kill *you*. . . . However annoying you are." The Saturday streets were almost empty; everyone was at home, watching the Derby on TV. Shane did not need to watch. Thanks to

Mo, he already knew the result. At least . . .

"You are quite sure, aren't you, Mo? You are quite, quite sure."

"Number Five, yes. Even now. Crossing the winning line," said Mo impatiently. "Listen . . . !"

But Shane was not listening. He was imagining what he would do with his winnings of £70. Perhaps he would buy himself a real mobile phone . . .

"*Owowo!*" wailed Mo. "*Danger! Danger! . . .Too late.*"

Bagless Dyson stepped out into their path. "My Dad lost his job. It's your fault," snarled Bagless. "You fixed it."

"No, no!"

"On that phone of yours."

"Futurescope," said Shane.

"Mobile."

"From Experimental Planet-Planet," said Shane. He took another step backwards. But the empty street behind him seemed to have filled up with people, and they all had noses, elbows and knees at about the same level as his. They were all angry.

"We want our money back," growled Class Four.

"Yes, yes! Let's pick up our winnings!" said Shane brightly. "I'm going to buy a *mobile phone* with mine!"

"You'll need one," said Knees, snatching Mo out of Shane's hand and raising his fist for the throw.

It was not that Number Five had *lost* the Derby exactly. She had won it by a clear six lengths.

On Planet-Planet.

"Oh YOUR Derby!" said Mo. "Why didn't you say so? I thought you meant OUR Derby! Back home. I could have told you Number Five would come in last down *here*."

Wapper snatched the phone from Knees, because he could throw better. He threw her into the street, where a large truck ran her over without so much as a warning toot.

Chapter Five
Mo Moans

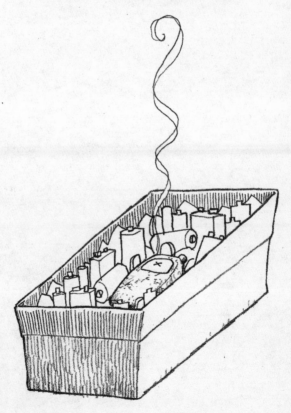

Mo's batteries were flat. They were as flat as after-dinner mints. So would yours be, if a truck ran over them.

Shane picked her up gently out of the road and cradled her in both hands. "Mo! Mo! Speak to me, Mo! Are you alright?"

"⊠ ⊠ ⊠ ⊠," blinked the luminous green screen, and then, "♎&♏◆ ◆❖⚹●⌂♐." It was all she could manage.

Shane made a cushion of soft toilet paper in a shoe-box and laid Mo in it for a bed. But though he talked to her all the while, in a soothing and encouraging way, Mo did not reply with so much as a scratching water buffalo or a revving scooter. All the heart seemed to have gone out of her, and along with it,

several computer circuits and her
amplifiers.

Class Four was embarrassed by
the sad little shoe box in Shane's
lap. They said no more about the
Derby or their lost pounds. They
were ashamed. Mo had, after all,
been able to tell the future, which
was pretty nifty. And now all she
could do was lie in a shoebox
showing the occasional chess move:
"Kp to B4" . . . or bridge hand.

From time to time, fragments of
future would drift through Mo's
circuits and she would talk of
shipwrecks, drip-dry toilet paper
and jet-packs, but her voice was no

louder than aged bees moaning softly about their rheumatism. Once, Shane heard a clickety-clack as soft as flies tap-dancing, and lifted the lid in time to see a text message on the dim, green screen.

♒♏●◻ ♓ ♋☽ ♎◹♓■♑✎

"Don't send," he told her tenderly. "They'll find you, remember? The people chasing you?" Not that he believed it, but he wanted Mo to know he cared about her safety. The picture of a battery appeared, tottered left and right, and fell off the screen into a luminous green abyss. "Batteries!" cried Shane. "Mo's dying!"

So Class Four took batteries out of their watches and their key-ring torches. Wapper took the battery out of his mobile phone (the one he was not supposed to have in school). They took batteries from their pocket calculators and mini-radios. They took the battery out of the classroom clock and had to sit through two hours of history before Mrs McKeckney realised that the clock had stopped. They took the battery from Donald's hearing aid and the battery from the electric pencil-sharpener on the front desk. But because they could not open Mo up, they had to settle for piling all these batteries around her in the shoe-box. Mo looked like a racing car taking a pit stop.

They took the batteries from their cycle lamps and from the TV remote-control. They even took the battery out of the smoke detector and threw it in on top of Mo, like a small, round, lifebelt.

Then Shane put the shoe-box lid back on and fastened it in place with a rubber band.

In Maths, he did not hear one word the teacher said; he was too busy listening for signs of life inside his book-locker. But though he heard Attila the rat running round inside his wheel, no sound came from the shoebox.

All through History, Shane strained his ears for a sound from inside his locker. But though he heard people playing rounders on the field outside and the sports teacher blowing his whistle, no sound came from the shoebox.

All through Art, Shane listened to the rising racket around him as Class Four forgot about Mo and pasted tissue paper and wool on to egg boxes. Time and again, he fingered the handle of his locker as he passed, tempted to open it and check on Mo. But he dared not do it. What if she was dead? What are the vital signs of an alien mobile? How would he know?

He hoped it would rain so that they would not have to go outside for sports. He wanted to keep vigil. A single bleat, one bar of opera; one sigh of pneumatic brakes would be enough to lift his gloom. But inside the locker, inside her shoe box, inside her sarcophagus of alkali batteries, Mo made no sound at all.

Only while they were out at sports – when the classroom was hushed and even Attila the Rat was asleep in his straw – was there a noise from Shane's locker. Donald was still in the classroom, because he had a sick note. And Donald might have heard the sound, too . . . if Class Four had not borrowed the battery out of his hearing aid.

It was a sort of crepitation at first, like rabbits spitting. Then it was a rap-tap rat-a-tatting, like a very tiny, very impatient postman. It grew to a rattling, like badly fitting teeth – then a sort of scrabbling, like pigeons trying to tap dance, a snap-slap-smack crackling, like water on a hotplate. When it reached the level of fire crackers at Chinese New Year, smoke began to trickle out from under the locker door.

The smoke alarm did not sound, of course, because Class Four had taken the battery out of it. The fire was only discovered when Donald looked up from his comic and screamed, "FIRE!"

"No one is to go back indoors!" exclaimed Mrs McKeckney, out on the field. But hearing a noise like rapid machine-gun fire –
"*What the – ?*" – she ducked down behind a parked car. So she did not see, through the thickly wreathing smoke, how Shane Curry clambered through a classroom window, ran to his locker, tugged open the door, drew out a burning cardboard shoe-box and threw it out of the open

window on to the grass.

Wapper whipped out his mobile phone and called the Fire Brigade. Afterwards, the Head Teacher's mouth thanked him for his quick thinking. But her eyes said something far less gracious about Wapper and his mobile phone.

Shane, meanwhile, sat among the butterfly bushes with the shoe-box in his lap, not daring to look. At last his fingers snapped the melted rubber band. The burned cardboard stained his hands. Beneath the charred lid, the box looked like a coffin full of metal confetti. Mo the Mobile (Experimental model NK/11⊠☐〰 with full Foresee-the-Future facility and a large array of other useless features) lay amid a

glittering snow of metal filings, her
green screen blinking.

"I ate them," said Mo crossly,
"but it was really hard getting the
wrappers off. Are you sure Kit-Kats
don't suffer?"

The whole school stood
shivering on the playing field,
waiting for permission to file back
indoors. Instead of giving Wapper
back his mobile, the Head Teacher
held it up wordlessly, between finger
and thumb, for everyone to see, then
dropped it into her pocket:
confiscated.

With a fizz and a phut like
opening a ring-pull can, Mo began
to tremble in Shane's hands. For a
brief second she had caught sight of
Wapper's phone, held aloft against a

lilac evening sky. A crimson circle
formed on her green screen, like a
chest wound made by an arrow. Her

whole silver casing blushed gold.

And she let out a piercing wolf whistle.

Chapter Six
Mo's Beau

"Oh woe is Mo," said Mo, and gave a sigh like a bouncy castle deflating. "So crude, but oh so beautiful!"

"You can't have him . . . it," said Shane yet again. "It belongs to Wapper."

"We'll elope."

"If you elope with Wapper's phone, Wapper will kill me," said Shane. "It's just an old cell phone, Mo. You could do better for yourself."

"Cellaphone . . . Is that his name? Ah, Cellaphone! I can see it now . . . " murmured Mo obstinately. "I can see it now!"

But that much was untrue. As a result of being flattened by a truck, Mo had lost her memory of the Future. She could no longer see what the Future held for a mobile phone in love. She could no longer see whether there was happiness or danger lurking around the next corner – or even a pillar box with its eyes too close together. Mo had become positively short-sighted. In fact she had eyes only for Wapper's mobile.

Now Wapper's mobile was not a piece of intelligent technology. Wapper was not intelligent, but alongside his mobile phone, he was Einstein with a Nobel Prize for Cleverness. His phone was simply a plastic casing, a SIM card, some printed circuitry and a battery.

"He has *lovely* keys!" breathed Mo. But Wapper's phone was not from Experimental Planet-Planet. It did not think, or speak Lingua Planet, or pulse with emotion, or do impressions, or play chess. And it could not return Mo's tender feelings.

There was one other small problem: Wapper's phone was in prison. The Head Teacher had locked it away in her desk, and did not intend to give it back until Easter.

That night, in bed, Shane could feel Mo trembling, all the way through the pillow. By three in the morning, her mind was made up. "We have to rescue him!"

"No, Mo," said Shane. He tried to make it sound final, like his Mother when she used a two-word sentence. But Mo had never had a mother – at least not one like Shane's.

Mo texted Wapper's phone to say that she was coming to rescue him. There was no reply. She transmitted it in Morse Code and in Braille, on long-wave, short-wave and via satellites hovering over the Indian Ocean. There was no reply.

"Perhaps you've got the wrong number!" Shane pleaded. But Mo – gazing into a lilac sky – had scanned the data in a space of a heartbeat, like a policeman memorising a number plate.

"I thought it was dangerous for you to transmit," said Shane, trying to restrain her. "I thought a posse from Planet-Planet would home in on you."

But Mo was past caring. "My safety doesn't matter. We have to rescue poor Cellaphone!"

She made up poetry and mailed that. There was no reply.

"Maybe it's flat!" begged Shane. "Maybe its . . . his batteries are dead!" But the word 'dead' only threw Mo into a grieving panic and she lifted up her voice and bayed like a wolf at full moon. He pressed down on the pillow; he piled the duvet on top, but his sister Cora still came tumbling into the room in her nightdress.

"Are you trying to wake the whole street?"

By the time he had explained it all, they were outside the school gates,

dressing gowns blowing in the wind,
Mo muffled between two pillows,
like a giant mobile sandwich.

"*Where are you, Cellaphone?
Where are you?*" came the muffled
cry. Mo shouted it in Latin and in

French. She shouted it in Esperanto and Martian. She howled it like a winter wind. She whistled, as if Wapper's phone were a sheep dog and might come running. And sometimes she raged like an angry hedge-trimmer on a Sunday morning.

Across the deserted playground the noise echoed and re-echoed. Neighbourhood dogs set up a grumpy bark-bark-bark. Lights went on in windows along the street.

As well as the noise, there were electrical impulses and rashes of magnetism. So, as Shane and Cora crept down the empty school corridors, between the coat pegs, overhead lights flickered on and off, and pieces of school equipment came mysteriously to life. In the cleaning cupboard a vacuum gave a throaty roar. Somewhere, a video machine began to record Open University. A computer screen lit up. The exercise wheel in Attila's cage began to turn of its own accord.

In nearby homes, electric blankets and toasters heated up.

Mo may have hidden her talents from Shane, but now she could not contain her genius. She was drunk on excitement and a-dazzle with data. Memories and thoughts flickered across walls, ceiling and floor, like brightness from a glitter-ball: images of fire, mahjong, a lilac sky, pillar boxes, pelican crossings and old English sheepdogs; pictures of deep (and shallow) Space, of

Planet-Planet, of her brother Meemo and of Number Five winning the Planet-Planet Derby. Text streamed out of her, in long green tentacles like some astral octopus.

The pillows began to scorch. Cora tossed them aside and pushed Mo deep into her dressing gown pocket instead . . . and her hair stood straight up on end and turned a luminous blue. "Fabidoccio!" said Cora. "Where did you steal this, bro? Can you get another one, for me?"

Shane tried to explain, yet again, about Experimental Planet-Planet and Mo's bid for freedom, but it was hard to make himself heard above the serenade from *Carmen* that Mo was singing:

"... *si je t'aime, prende garde a toi!*"

(Naturally, since the accident with the truck, Mo sang very, very flat.)

On the walls, the fire extinguishers began to flex their short hoses; blossoms of foam fell on the carpet tiles. Then all the car alarms in the street outside went off and the street lamps began to revolve like searchlights.

"Control yourself, Mo!" said Shane. "Get a grip!" But the alien was busy scouring the airwaves for a reply from her sweetheart. Music and crackle and foreign stations and World Service Radio poured out of her, rattling the glass in the window frames.

Once inside the Head Teacher's office, Mo bleeped like a metal detector in a tin can factory. The metal bookshelves jitterbugged in Mo's magnetic force field. Cora and Shane slid open the long desk drawer and at last found Wapper's phone, along with a confiscated pack of cards, a Game Boy, some chewing gum and a Swiss Army penknife.

"Hello! Hello! Hello!" bellowed Mo at her inamorato. Cora passed Mo to Shane, and switched on the cell phone.

"Give it us!" said a voice like a dollop of tarmac. "Thas mine, that!"

Wapper, in his Star Wars pyjamas and Zorro mask, squeezed through the window of the Head

Teacher's office, his torch beam
glinting like a blade. Behind him
came Bagless and Knees. They had
come to get back Wapper's
confiscated phone, only to find it in
the sticky grasp of Shane Curry.

"Give it over," said Knees, making a fist. "It's Wapper's mum's and she'll kill 'im if she don't get it back."

The metal filing cabinet opened its top drawer and fell over on its face. The table lamp flickered dimly, like a deep-sea life form. The pump in the fish tank churned the water into a seething maelstrom.

"*Amo! Amo! Amo!*" said Mo, beseechingly, bypassing her beloved's SIM code.

"Don't mess with me, Shane Curry," warned Bagless. "I'll tell my dad on you."

Cora Curry put on her most sneering mouth and fearless feet. The swirling streetlights flickered off her braces. "Your dad knows you're here then, does he, Bagless Dyson?"

"*O Willow, willow, willow, willow!*" whispered Mo. "Speak to me, dearest!"

LOW BATTERY
said the message on Wapper's

phone. It looked like a rude remark.

Now Wapper's cell phone was not a piece of intelligent technology. Wapper was not intelligent, but in comparison with his cell phone, he was Clever Pie with an extra side-serving of brains. Confused by all the static electricity crackling around the room, Wapper's cell phone vibrated, fell out of Shane's hand, struck the corner of the desk, dialled Last Number Called . . . and accidentally summoned the Fire Brigade again.

Chapter Seven
Mo Go

The Police came too – not in answer to Wapper's phone but because of all the complaints they were getting from the neighbourhood: about lights and noise and rogue toasters popping.

At the sound of the sirens, Cora and Shane fled. They dived out of the open office window into the shrubbery. Bagless and Knees would have followed, but they spent too long quarrelling about who should go first. Somehow the window got broken in the struggle. Then they noticed that Wapper was not with them and pulled in their heads again, hissing, "Whatya doing, Wapper?"

More afraid of his mother than of the police, Wapper was still crawling about under the Head's desk, looking for his mobile.

"Wapper! Leave it! Let's get out of here!"

A fire engine, its klaxon blaring, roared into the street scattering cats and litter. Blinded by a sudden flash of light, its driver struck the police car a glancing blow, spinning it round. Hose unwound from the fire-pump like a startled python. The policemen were confused – both by the flash of light and by the jarring jolt. But they were even more confused when all the street lights suddenly went out. So they forgot to arrest the driver of the fire engine and simply stood about amid the coils of fire-hose, blinking their eyes, trying to get their bearings in the treacly dark.

And by the time their eyes adjusted, the school had gone.

Shane and Cora saw it go – saw the concrete peel itself off the ground and rise into the air. They saw the underside of the floorboards, the pipes kinking between all the radiators. They heard the furniture skidding to and fro as the school banked to the right and rose skywards. They heard the slurping noise of tractor-beams sucking up Pond Street Primary School as if it was a single strand of spaghetti.

Shane made a grab at one of the drainpipes – *"Wapper! Knees! Get out of there! Jump!"* – and was lifted several metres into the air. But

Cora caught hold of his feet, her weight prising his fingers free, and he dropped back down into the bushes. A marker pen, a football sock and an empty rat's cage fell on top of him.

As for the rest, there was nothing left – nothing! – except a deeper darkness in the shape of a primary school – such as a finger might draw in a steamy bathroom mirror.

Fire Brigade and Police decided they had taken a wrong turning. Schools don't simply disappear. So finding no school at the end of the darkened street, they decided they were in the wrong street, and headed back to the ring road.

Then calls started to come in from all over town – ridiculous hoax calls about space ships and lights in the sky and other such nonsense. The Police were so annoyed, and the Fire Brigade so sniggery, that the earlier call-out was forgotten. By the time somebody said, "Shouldn't we be getting over to Pond Street?" . . . it was daylight and everything was much easier to find.

And there was Pond Street Primary School. In Pond Street. As it generally was. It seemed to be facing in a slightly different direction from usual. But schools don't roll over in the night like sleeping dogs. So the Police – and the teachers and the children and the neighbours – decided it was a trick of the light and took no notice.

There was Mrs McKeckney on playground duty. There was the caretaker mending a window. There were the netball posts and parked cars and the shrubbery. There were Years Three, Five and Six ranging up and down behind the railings, like animals in a zoo. There were the children of Class Four, lying on their backs on the football pitch, staring up at the sky. Everything was quite normal, in fact.

It is true that Bagless, Wapper and Knees had been found, at three in the morning, marooned at the top of a telegraph pole five miles out of town, but then *those* three were

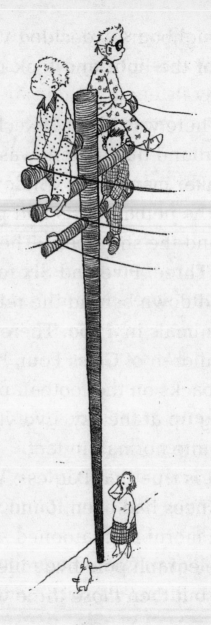

always doing stupid things, so nobody was terribly surprised. And nobody listened to their far-fetched excuses for being up there.

"They got Mo then?" said Gigi, biting her lip. "She said They were after her."

Shane nodded sadly. He was perfectly sure there was nothing left in the Head Teacher's desk drawer this morning but a pack of cards, a Game Boy, a Swiss Army Knife and a dead goldfish. "I didn't believe her! I told her she was safe! I said They'd never come looking for her here!" Shane blamed himself.

"Do you think They took her back to Planet-Planet?" said Chiller, with chilling gloom.

Shane nodded again, tragedy written all over his face. "She was too talented to be allowed to escape and make a life for herself."

"But she couldn't do nuffing," Smiler pointed out. "She was useless." Shane glared at her.

"Never mind her. What about Wapper and Knees and me?" said Bagless in a low moan. It was the first time anyone had heard him speak since his return to Earth. "What if They stole our brains while we were . . . *up there* . . .and turned us into robots and we don't know it yet!"

"Well, do you *remember* them stealing your brains?"

"Nah, but we wouldn't, would

we?" said Knees, his face twisting as he struggled to work it out. "'Cos we'd have nowhere to remember it in."

"Well, what *do* you remember?" asked Gigi patiently.

Slow-motion, action-replay scenes looped again and again through Bagless' head . . . alien screwdrivers dismantling the school piece by piece, alien antennae homing in on the Head Teacher's desk; alien jaws chewing on chewing gum; the rattle of a cage . . . "Poor Attila," said Bagless.

Gigi sighed. "If you were converted into a robot, Bagless, you'd be really clever now," she said. Class Four looked Bagless Dyson over and decided he had not been turned into an alien robot. He was still just Bagless.

"They could've given us a free phone, at least, while we was up there!" said Knees sulkily. "Got plenty! Never seen so many!" Instead, Knees had no souvenirs of his journey into space, except for a lingering dose of travel sickness.

"Mum's gonna kill me," said Wapper. He had said it many times already. For the fact was, the aliens of Experimental Planet-Planet had not only recaptured Mo the Mobile; they had shanghaied Wapper's mum's cell phone, too – not to mention Attila the Rat – whisking them away to a life of unimaginable horrors somewhere between Beta Centauri and *Wow!* in the constellation of the Flying Zebra.

Chapter Eight
No Mo

The text message came through on Shane's computer. (It couldn't come through on his telephone, because he didn't have one.) The text said:

"PCK P SHN WHT KPT U? HW M SPPSD T SPK WTH U F U DNT GT PHN? HPPY T B HM. PLNT-PLNT HPPY T GT M BCK. NW HPPYM™ MCRCHP NSRTD. HPPY M! HPPY HPPY HPPY. DMG LL MNDD NW. MR FNCTNS DDD. LL TSTS PSSD. M GNG NT PRDCTN. BG SLS XPCTD THNKS T NW HPPYM ND BLT-N FX MCHN. HPPY M! HPPY HPPY HPPY.

CLLPHN WS CNVRTD . . ."

Shane looked at the message for a few minutes, and at the cursor winking brightly in the corner of the screen, daring him to delete. After a while, Shane typed his reply:

"Pardon?"

A box popped up on the screen.

Instructions for use

Just add water.
And vowels.

So Shane printed out the message and put it in a bucket of water with a sprinkling of vowels. It helped.

"PICK UP, SHANE! WHAT KEPT U? HOW AM I SUPPOSED TO SPEAK WITH U IF U DON'T GET A PHONE? HAPPY TO BE HOME. PLANET-PLANET HAPPY TO GET ME BACK. NEW HAPPYMO™ MICROCHIP INSERTED. HAPPY MO! HAPPY

HAPPY HAPPY.
DAMAGE ALL MENDED
NOW. MORE FUNCTIONS
ADDED. ALL TESTS PASSED. MO
GOING INTO PRODUCTION. BIG
SALES EXPECTED THANKS TO

NEW HAPPYMO™ MICROCHIP
AND BUILT-IN FAX MACHINE.
HAPPY MO. HAPPY, HAPPY,
HAPPY!

CELLAPHONE WAS
CONVERTED . . ."

A small thud of fear kicked
Shane in the ribs. What had They
done to Mo to bring about this
unlikely cheerfulness? What had
They done to Wapper's poor simple
cell phone, so lost, so alone, so out-
of-place on Experimental Planet-
Planet?

Behind him, Cora came into the
room. Her eyes darted over the
screen. Her hands shot over his
shoulders and typed the response,
"CONVERTED? WHAT RELIGION
IS HE NOW, THEN?"

Green thought bubbles drifted thoughtfully across the screen.

"CELLAPHONE CONVERTED INTO STATE-OF-THE-ART ORACLE-OF-DELPHI™ FUTUREPHONE™ WITH PAY-AS-U-GO, SIMPLE-TO-USE 'GENIUS'™ SLOT-IN CARD. HE IS JUST SO ADVANCED! BUT HE LOVES ME! YES, HE LOVES ME! EVEN THOUGH HE IS SO MUCH CLEVERER! O HAPPY MO! HAPPY, HAPPY, HAPPY!

. . . THIS TEXTING TAKES AN AGE, CURRY. GET YOUR MOTHER TO BUY U A MOBILE!"

Cora's elbows rested heavy on Shane' shoulders as she pondered how to ask Mo for two free samples from Planet-Planet.

But Shane pushed his chair back sharply, stood up like a piano player in a jazz club, and rattled off a state-of-the-art, pay-as-you-go, simple-to-use, two-word answer:

"NO WAY!"

That was that, he thought, until a sudden terrible afterthought struck him and he simply had to add:

"P.S. WHAT HAPPENED TO ATTILA?"

They waited a minute for the answer. Words took time to ping through the universe, bouncing off space litter and meteorites, scorching their way through re-entry.

Then Shane read the answer and smiled. Class Four would be

happy, happy, happy to hear it.

"FLIGHT CAPTAIN ATTILA AWARDED MEDAL LAST WEEK FOR SERVICES TO SCIENCE. WHAT A BRAIN!"

Geraldine McCaughrean

writes books for readers of
all ages. She has won many prizes,
including the Whitbread Children's
Award, the Library Association
Carnegie Medal, the Guardian
Award and the Blue Peter Book of the
Year Award.
She has also retold hundreds of
myths, legends, folktales
and literary classics.